CIRCUS FUN

Margaret Hillert

Illustrated by ELAINE RAPHAEL

FOLLETT PUBLISHING COMPANY
chicago

Library of Congress Catalog Card Number: 69-15968

ISBN 0-695-31487-4 Paper edition
ISBN 0-695-41487-7 Library edition

Eleventh Printing

CIRCUS FUN

Oh, Father, look, look.
Here is something funny.
I want to go to it.

Father said, "Come, come.
We can go.
Run, run, run."

I see it.
Here it is.
We go in here.

Here is something big.

Big, big, big.

It can work.

It can help.

See it make something go up.
Something red and blue and yellow.
Oh, my.
We want to go in.

11

Here we go, Father.

Up, here, up here.

Help me go up.

I see something.

I want something.

I want a red one.

13

Oh, look, look.

One little one.

Two big ones.

See the blue ball.

The little one can play ball.

See something funny.

It can go up.

It can come down.

Up and down.

Up and down.

Oh, oh, oh.

Look up here.

Look up and up and up.

And look down here.

Here is something big.

It is yellow.

It wants to jump and play.

Here is a funny one.

I see three balls.

Red, yellow, and blue balls.

Oh, oh.

Where is the red ball?

Where is the yellow ball?

Where is the blue ball?

Here is one.

Here is one.

And — here is one.

See my funny car.

Come into my funny car.

We can go away in it.

Away, away, away.

Look here.

See the big father.

See the big mother.

See the little baby.

You can go up.

I can help you go up.

Up you go.

24

Oh, Father, Father.

See me.

See me.

It is fun up here.

Down.

Down.

Down I come.

Mother, Mother.

Look here.

Here is something for you.

And here is a cookie for you.
Cookies for you and Father.

Follett JUST Beginning-To-Read Books

Uses of these books. These books are planned for the very youngest readers, those who have been learning to read for about six to eight weeks and who have a small preprimer reading vocabulary. The books are written by Margaret Hillert, a first-grade teacher in the Royal Oak, Michigan, schools. Each book is illustrated in full color.

Children will have a feeling of accomplishment in their first reading experiences with these delightful books that they can read.

CIRCUS FUN

A boy and his father have an eventful and exciting day at the circus, told in 50 preprimer words.

Word List

6 oh

father

look

here

is

something

funny

I

want (s)

to

go

it

8 said

come

we

can

run

9 see

in

10 big

work

help

11 make

up

red

and

blue

yellow

my

12 me

13 a

one (s)

14 little

two

the

ball (s)

play

15 down

18 jump

19 three

20 where

22 car

into

away

23 mother

baby

24 you

25 fun

28 for

29 cookie (s)